THE WILD WOOD
and
MOLE'S CHRISTMAS

Abridged from the original story by
KENNETH GRAHAME

Illustrated by E.H. Shepard

METHUEN CHILDREN'S BOOKS

The Wind in the Willows originally published
8th October 1908 by Methuen & Co Ltd
The Wild Wood and Mole's Christmas first published
in this format 1991 by Methuen Children's Books
A Division of the Octopus Publishing Group
Michelin House, 81 Fulham Road, London SW3 6RB
Text copyright © 1991 Methuen Children's Books
This presentation copyright © 1991 Methuen Children's Books
Line illustrations by Ernest H. Shepard
copyright under the Berne Convention
Colouring of the illustrations copyright © 1970, 1971
by Ernest H. Shepard and Methuen Children's Books Ltd.

Printed in Hong Kong by Wing King Tong

ISBN 0 416 16702 0

THE WILD WOOD

The Mole had long wanted to make the acquaintance of the Badger. He seemed to be such an important personage. But whenever the Mole mentioned his wish to the Water Rat he always found himself put off.

"Couldn't you ask him here – dinner or something?" said the Mole.

"He wouldn't come," replied the Rat simply. "Badger hates Society, and invitations, and all that sort of thing."

"Well, then, supposing we go and call on *him*," suggested the Mole.

"O, I'm sure he wouldn't like that at *all*," said the Rat, quite alarmed. "He's so very shy, he'd be sure to be offended. Besides, we can't. He lives in the very middle of the Wild Wood."

The Mole had to be content with this and it was not till summer was long over, and cold and frost kept them much indoors, that he found his thoughts dwelling again on the solitary grey Badger, who lived his own life by himself, in the middle of the Wild Wood.

In the winter time the Rat slept a great deal. During his short day he scribbled poetry or did small domestic jobs about the house and, of course, there were always animals dropping in for a chat.

Still the Mole had a good deal of spare time on his hands, and so one afternoon, when the Rat in his armchair was alternately dozing and trying over rhymes that wouldn't fit, he formed the resolution to go out and explore the Wild Wood, and perhaps strike up an acquaintance with Mr Badger.

It was a cold still afternoon with a hard steely sky overhead, when he slipped out of the warm parlour into the open air. The country lay bare and entirely leafless around him. With great cheerfulness of spirit he pushed on towards the Wild Wood, which lay before him low and threatening.

There was nothing to alarm him at first. Twigs crackled under his feet, logs tripped him, funguses on stumps startled him for a moment, but that was all fun, and exciting.

Then the faces began.

He thought he saw a little evil face, looking out at him from a hole. He quickened his pace, telling himself cheerfully not to begin imagining things, or there would be simply no end to it. He passed another hole, and another; and then – yes! – no! – yes! certainly a little narrow face flashed up and was gone. He hesitated – and strode on. Then suddenly there were hundreds of them, coming and going rapidly, all hard-eyed and evil and sharp.

Then the whistling began.

Very faint and shrill it was, and far behind him, when first he heard it.

Then it broke out on either side. They were up and alert and ready, whoever they were! And he was alone, and far from help and the night was closing in.

Then the pattering began.

Was it in front or behind? It seemed to be closing in on him, hunting, chasing something or – somebody? In panic, he began to run too. He ran up against things, he fell over things and into things. At last he took refuge in the deep dark hollow of an old beech tree.

He was too tired to run any further and could only snuggle down into the dry leaves and hope he was safe.

Meantime the Rat, warm and comfortable, dozed by his fireside. Then a coal slipped, the fire crackled and he woke with a start. He reached down to the floor for his verses, and then looked  round for the Mole to ask him if he knew a rhyme for something or other. But the Mole was not there. He called "Moly!" several times, and, receiving no answer, got up and went out into the hall. The Mole's cap and goloshes were gone.

The Rat left the house hoping to find the Mole's tracks. There they were, sure enough. He could see the imprints in the mud, leading direct to the Wild Wood. The Rat looked very grave.

Then he re-
entered the house,
strapped a belt
round his waist,
shoved a brace of
pistols into it,
took up a stout cudgel and set off for the
Wild Wood at a smart pace.

Here and there wicked little faces
popped out of holes, but vanished
immediately at sight of the valorous
animal, his pistols and the great ugly
cudgel in his grasp. He made his way
through the length of the wood, all the
time calling out cheerfully, "Moly, Moly,
Moly! Where are you? It's me – old Rat!"

At last to his joy he heard a feeble voice, saying, "Ratty! Is that really you?" The Rat crept into the hollow, and there he found the Mole, exhausted and still trembling. "O Rat!" he cried, "I've been so frightened!"

"O, I quite understand," said the Rat soothingly. "You shouldn't really have gone and done it, Mole. I did my best to keep you from it."

"Surely Mr Toad wouldn't mind coming here by himself?" inquired the Mole.

"Toad?" said the Rat, laughing. "He wouldn't show his face here alone, not for a whole hatful of golden guineas."

The Mole was greatly cheered by the Rat's laughter and the sight of his stick and his gleaming pistols.

"Now, then," said the Rat, "we really must make a start for home. It will never do to spend the night here."

"Dear Ratty," said the poor Mole. "You must let me rest here a while longer, if I'm to get home at all."

"O, all right," said the good-natured Rat, "rest away."

When the Mole woke up, the Rat went to the entrance of their retreat and put his head out. Then the Mole heard him saying quietly to himself, "Hullo! hullo! here – *is* – a – go!"

"What's up, Ratty?" asked the Mole.

"*Snow* is up," replied the Rat briefly, "or rather, *down*. It's snowing hard."

The Mole crouched beside him, and, looking out, saw a gleaming carpet springing up everywhere. A fine powder filled the air and caressed the cheek.

"Well, well, it can't be helped," said the Rat. "We must make a start. The worst of it is, this snow makes everything look so very different."

They set out bravely, and took the line that seemed most promising. An hour or two later they pulled up, dispirited, weary, and hopelessly at sea. The snow was so deep that they could hardly drag their little legs through it. There seemed to be no way out.

"Look here," said the Rat. "There's a sort of dell down there. We'll make our way down into that, and try and find some sort of shelter."

They struggled down and hunted about for a corner that was dry.

Suddenly the Mole tripped up and fell forward on his face with a squeal.

"O, my leg!" he cried. "O my poor shin!"

"Poor old Mole!" said the Rat kindly. "Let's have a look."

"I must have tripped over a hidden branch," said the Mole miserably.

"It's a very clean cut," said the Rat. "Looks as if it was made by a sharp edge of something in metal. Funny!"

"Well, never mind what done it," said the Mole, forgetting his grammar in his pain. "It hurts just the same."

But the Rat had left him and was busy scraping in the snow.

Suddenly he cried, "Hooray!" and then, "Hooray-ooray-ooray-ooray!" and fell to executing a feeble jig in the snow.

"What *have* you found, Ratty?" asked the Mole.

"Come and see!" said the delighted Rat.

The Mole hobbled up and had a good look. "A door-scraper! Well, what of it? Why dance jigs round a door-scraper?"

"But don't you just see what it *means*, you – you dull-witted animal?" cried the Rat impatiently. And he set to work again and made the snow fly all around him. After some further toil, a very shabby door-mat lay exposed to view.

"There, what did I tell you?" exclaimed the Rat in triumph.

"Absolutely nothing," replied the Mole. "Can we *eat* a door-mat? Or sleep under a door-mat, you exasperating rodent?"

"Do – you – mean – to – say," cried the excited Rat, "that this door-mat doesn't *tell* you anything? Scrape and dig if you want to sleep dry and warm tonight, for it's our last chance!"

The Rat attacked a snow-bank beside them, digging with fury; and the Mole scraped busily too, to oblige the Rat. At last, the result of their labours stood full in view of the astonished Mole. In the side of what had seemed to be a snow-bank stood a solid little door. On a small brass plate, neatly engraved, they could read:

MR BADGER

The Mole fell backwards from sheer surprise. "Rat!" he cried, "You're a wonder! If I only had your head —"

"But as you haven't," interrupted the Rat rather unkindly, "get up at once and hang on to that bell-pull and ring as hard as you can, while I hammer!"

While the Rat attacked the door with his stick, the Mole sprang up at the bell-pull, clutched it and swung there, both his feet well off the ground, and from quite a long way off they could faintly hear a deep-toned bell respond.

They waited patiently for what seemed a very long time. At last they heard the sound of slow shuffling footsteps. There was the noise of a bolt shot back,

and the door opened a few inches.

"Now, the *very* next time this happens," said a gruff voice, "I shall be exceedingly angry. Who is it?"

"O, Badger," cried the Rat, "It's me, Rat, and my friend Mole, and we've lost our way in the snow."

"What, Ratty, my dear little man!" exclaimed the Badger, in quite a different voice. "Come along in, both of you. Why, you must be perished."

The two animals tumbled over each other in their eagerness to get inside. The Badger looked kindly down on them and patted both their heads. "This is not the sort of night for small animals to be out," he said. "Come along into the kitchen.

"There's a first-rate fire there, and supper and everything."

He shuffled on in front of them and they followed him down a long, gloomy passage, into the glow and warmth of a large fire-lit kitchen. The oaken settles exchanged cheerful glances with each other; plates on the dresser grinned at pots on the shelf, and the merry firelight flickered and played over everything. The kindly Badger thrust them down on a settle to toast themselves at the fire and bathed the Mole's shin and mended the cut with sticking-plaster till the whole thing was just as good as new, if not better.

When they were thoroughly toasted, the Badger summoned them to the table. When they saw the supper that was spread for them, really it seemed only a question of what they should attack first.

Conversation was impossible for a long time; and when it was slowly resumed, it was that regrettable sort of conversation that results from talking with your mouth full. The Badger did not mind that sort of thing at all, nor did he take any notice of elbows on the table, or everybody speaking at once. He nodded gravely as the animals told their story; and he did not seem surprised or shocked at anything, and he never said, "I told you so," or remarked that they ought to have done so-and-so. The Mole began to feel very friendly towards him.

When supper was finished at last, they gathered round the fire and the Badger said heartily, "Now then! tell us the news. How's old Toad going on?"

"O, from bad to worse," said the Rat gravely. "Another smash-up only last week. This is the seventh."

"He's been in hospital three times," put in the Mole; "and as for the fines he's had to pay, it's awful to think of!"

"Yes," continued the Rat. "Toad's rich, but he's not a millionaire. And he's a hopelessly bad driver. Badger! We're his friends – oughtn't we to do something?"

The Badger went through a bit of hard thinking. "Now look here!" he said at last. "You know I can't do anything now?"

His two friends assented. No animal is ever expected to do anything strenuous or heroic during the winter. "But," continued the Badger, "once the year has really turned, then we'll take the Toad seriously in hand. We'll make him be a sensible Toad. You're asleep, Rat!"

"Not me!" said the Rat, waking up with a jerk.

"He's been asleep two or three times since supper," said the Mole, laughing.

"Well, it's time we were all in bed," said the Badger. "I'll show you your quarters. And take your time tomorrow – breakfast at any hour you please!"

The two tired animals came down to breakfast very late next morning, and found two young hedgehogs sitting on a bench, eating porridge.

"Where's Mr Badger?" inquired the Mole.

"The master's gone into his study, sir," replied a hedgehog. "He said he was going to be particular busy this morning."

This explanation was understood by everyone present. The animals well knew that Badger, having eaten a hearty breakfast, had retired to his study, settled in an armchair and was being "busy" in the usual way at this time of year.

The front-door bell clanged loudly and in walked the Otter.

"Thought I should find you here," he said cheerfully. "They were in a state of alarm along the River Bank this morning. Rat never been home all night – nor Mole either. But I knew that when people were in any fix they mostly went to Badger, so I came straight here, through the Wild Wood."

"Weren't you at all – er – nervous?" asked the Mole.

The Otter showed a gleaming set of strong white teeth as he laughed. "I'd give 'em nerves if any of them tried anything on with me."

Just then Badger entered, yawning and rubbing his eyes, and they all sat down to luncheon together. The Mole took the opportunity to tell Badger how home-like it all felt to him. "Once well underground," he said, "nothing can get at you."

The Badger beamed on him. "That's exactly what I say," he replied. "And then, if your ideas get larger, a dig and a scrape and there you are! If you feel your house is a bit too big, you stop up a hole or two. No builders, no tradesmen and, above all, no weather. When lunch is over, I'll take you round this little place of mine."

So after luncheon, Badger lighted a lantern and bade the Mole follow him.

The Mole was staggered at the size of it all. "How on earth," he said, "did you find time and strength to do all this?"

"As a matter of fact I did none of it — only cleaned out the passages," said the Badger simply. "You see very long ago, there was a city of people here."

"But what has become of them all?" asked the Mole.

"Who can tell?" said the Badger. "People come and go. But we remain. Badgers are an enduring lot."

When they got
back to the kitchen
again, they found
the Rat walking up
and down, very
restless. He seemed
to be afraid that the
river would run away
if he wasn't there to
look after it.

"Come along,
Mole," he said anxiously.
"We must get off. Don't want to spend
another night in the Wild Wood."

"It'll be all right," said the Otter. "I'm
coming with you, and if there's a head
that needs to be punched, you can
confidently rely upon me to punch it."

"You needn't fret, Ratty," added the
Badger placidly. "When you have to go,
you shall leave by one of my short cuts."

The Rat was nevertheless still anxious to be off, so the Badger led the way along a damp and airless tunnel for a distance that seemed to be miles. At last daylight began to show through the mouth of the passage. The Badger, bidding them good-bye, pushed them through the opening and retreated.

They found themselves standing on the very edge of the Wild Wood: rocks and brambles and tree-roots behind them, in front quiet fields and, far ahead, a glint of the familiar old river.

MOLE'S
CHRISTMAS

Some days later, Mole and Rat were
returning across country after a long day's
outing with Otter. The shades of the
short winter day were closing in, and they
had still some distance to go.

They plodded along steadily and
silently, each of them thinking his own
thoughts. The Rat was walking a little
way ahead, as his habit was, his eyes fixed
on the straight grey road in front of him;
so he did not notice poor Mole when
suddenly the summons reached him, and
took him like an electric shock.

It was a mysterious call that suddenly reached Mole in the darkness, making him tingle through and through with its very familiar appeal, even while as yet he could not clearly remember what it was. He stopped dead in his tracks, his nose searching hither and thither. A moment, and he had caught it again; and with it came recollection in fullest flood.

Home! That was what they meant, those caressing appeals, wafted through the air! Why, it must be quite close by him at that moment, his old home that he had hurriedly forsaken that day when he first found the river! Since his escape on that bright morning he had hardly given it a thought. Now, with a rush of old memories, how clearly it stood up before him in the darkness!

"Ratty!" he called, full of joyful excitement, "hold on! Come back!"

"O, *come* along, Mole, do!" replied the Rat cheerfully, still plodding along.

"*Please* stop, Ratty!" pleaded the poor Mole, in anguish. "You don't understand! It's my old home! I've just come across the smell of it. I *must* go to it, I must. Please, please come back!"

The Rat was very far ahead, too far to hear clearly what the Mole was calling.

"Mole, we mustn't stop now, really!" he called back. "It's late and the snow's coming on again."

Poor Mole stood in the road, his heart torn asunder. But his loyalty to his friend stood firm. With an effort he caught up the unsuspecting Rat, who began chattering cheerfully about what they would do when they got back, never noticing his companion's silence and distress. At last, however, he stopped and said kindly, "Look here, Mole old chap, you seem dead tired. We'll sit down for a minute and rest."

The Mole subsided forlornly on a tree-stump. The sob he had fought with so long refused to be beaten and he cried freely and helplessly and openly.

The Rat, astonished and dismayed, did not dare to speak for a while. At last he said, very quietly, "What is it, old fellow? Whatever is the matter?"

Poor Mole found it difficult to get any words out.

"I know it's a — shabby, dingy little place," he sobbed at last, "but it was my own little home — and I was fond of it and I smelt it suddenly when I called and you wouldn't listen, Rat — and everything came back to me with a rush — and I *wanted* it! — O dear, O dear!"

The Rat stared straight in front of him saying nothing. After a time he muttered gloomily, "I see it all now! What a *pig* I have been! A pig — that's me!" Then he rose from his seat, and, remarking carelessly, "Well, now we'd really better be getting on, old chap!" set off up the road again, over the toil-some way they had come.

"Wherever are you (hic) going to (hic), Ratty?" cried the tearful Mole.

"We're going to find that home of yours," replied the Rat pleasantly. "You had better come along. It will take some finding, and we shall want your nose."

They moved on in silence for some little way, when suddenly Mole stood rigid, while his uplifted nose, quivering slightly, felt the air. Suddenly, without warning, Mole dived and Rat followed him down the tunnel to which his nose had faithfully led him.

Facing them was Mole's little front door.

Mole's face beamed. He lit a lamp, and took one glance round his old home. He saw the dust lying thick on everything, the deserted look of the neglected house — and collapsed on a chair. "O Ratty!" he cried. "Why did I bring you to this poor, cold little place!"

The Rat paid no heed. "What a capital little house this is!" he called out cheerily. "We'll make a jolly night of it. First we want a good fire." The Rat soon had a cheerful blaze roaring, but Mole had another fit of the blues.

"Rat," he moaned, "how about your supper? I've nothing to give you."

"What a fellow you are for giving in!" said the Rat reproachfully. "Come with me and forage."

They went and foraged and found a tin of sardines, a box of biscuits and a German sausage.

"There's a banquet for you!" observed the Rat.

"No bread!" groaned the Mole, "No butter, no –"

"No *pâté de foie gras*, no champagne!" continued the Rat, grinning.

He had just got to work with the sardine-opener when sounds were heard from the fore-court.

"What's up?" inquired the Rat.

"It must be the field-mice," replied the Mole. "They go round carol-singing regularly at this time of year."

"Let's have a look at them!" cried the Rat, running to the door.

In the fore-court stood some eight or ten little field-mice. They glanced shyly at each other, sniggering a little, and their little voices uprose on the air.

"Well sung, boys!" cried the Rat heartily when the voices ceased. "Now come along in and warm yourselves."

"Yes, come along," cried the Mole eagerly. "Now, you just wait a minute, while we – O Ratty!" he cried in despair. "We've nothing to give them!"

"You leave all that to me," said the Rat. "Here, you with the lantern! Are there any shops open at this hour?"

"Why, certainly, sir," replied the field-mouse. Much muttered conversation ensued. Finally, there was a chink of coins, the field-mouse was provided with a basket and off he hurried. The rest of the field-mice perched in a row on the settle and toasted their chilblains.

Soon the field-mouse with the lantern reappeared, staggering under the weight of his basket. Under the generalship of Rat, everybody was set to do something or to fetch something. In a very few minutes supper was ready, and Mole saw his little friends' faces brighten and beam as they fell to without delay; and then let himself loose on the provender, thinking what a happy home-coming this had turned out, after all.

When the door had closed on the last of them, the Rat, with a tremendous yawn, said, "Mole, old chap, I'm ready to drop," and he clambered into his bunk and rolled himself up in the blankets. The weary Mole also was glad to turn in. But ere he closed his eyes he let them wander round his old room. He did not want to abandon his new life, to turn his back on sun and air. But it was good to think he had this to come back to, this place which was all his own and could always be counted upon for the same simple welcome.